Scatterbrain Sam

English edition copyright © 1992 by The Child's World, Inc.
French edition © 1988 by Casterman
All rights reserved. No part of this book may be
reproduced or utilized in any form or by any means
without written permission from the Publisher.
Printed in the United States of America.

Distributed to schools and libraries
in Canada by
SAUNDERS BOOK CO.
Box 308
Collingwood, Ontario, Canada L9Y 3Z7
(800) 461-9120

ISBN 089565-754-6
Library of Congress Cataloging-in-Publication Data
available upon request

Scatterbrain Sam

author: Lucien Guy and Claude-Rose Touati
illustrator: Corderoc'h

The Child's World
Mankato, Minnesota

"Sam! Where are you? Hurry up, it's time for your flute lesson!"

Mama peeps into Sam's room. The big teddy bear is hiding his head under the pillow, but there's no sign of Sam.

"Wherever can he be?" sighs Mama.

He's not in the bathroom or the kitchen. The scamp always manages to vanish into thin air.

There's nothing ghost-like about Sam, however. He's a normal seven-year-old with sturdy legs and rumpled brown hair.

Mama looks at the clock: almost nine o'clock. Sam has to be at Miss Suzanne's house by nine-thirty. It takes a good half hour to get there.

Miss Suzanne lives in Purlow, a village about a mile and a half from Sam's house. Of course, Sam could walk faster if he chose, but he just cannot hurry. He hates to hurry. He likes to day-dream. Daydreams take up a lot of time; you just can't hurry them. They're fragile things, and break very easily.

Mama's coming down the garden path. Against the wall at the bottom of the garden, is the hut that Sam and his brother built. It's his favorite place. Mama comes up quietly, and suddenly she hears:

"Hello! Hello! Cosmos calling. Receiving you loud and clear. Over."

Mama hides in the shadow of the walnut tree and answers:

"Hello! Planet Mama calling. Captain Cosmos, you must not forget the flute lesson. Please hurry."

Startled, Sam pokes his head out of the hut window.

"Mama! It's you! Ohmigosh! My lesson! I forgot…"

"Go on, then, quickly, little scatterbrain! Grab your bag — ge going, or you'll be late!"

Sam runs to give his mother a kiss — a big "smack" on the cheek — runs up to his room, grabs his bag, runs all along the road, shouting "Charge, Cosmos!" at the top of his voice.

To get to Purlow, you have to cross over at the
crossroads by the farm. The crossing is not marked and
people have to manage by themselves. There are no
more dangerous places after that. Sam has no problems
along the way, and is soon in the shade of the woods.

This is a peaceful forest where the trees are full of
songbirds. Sam turns a couple of cartwheels, whistling
to himself — and he's Captain Cosmos again, off on a
mission to a distant planet. He enters a mysterious
region inhabited by strange creatures called tyrannias.

Suddenly a tyrannia appears in front of him, in the very middle of the clearing. The creature gives a terrible roar, and its huge red mouth opens wide, showing its pitiless great fangs. In one bound, Sam throws down his bag and is up on a half-buried, mossy tree trunk, brandishing a dry branch that turns into a stick of dynamite.

"All together now, brother tyrannias, we'll take on Cosmos!"

"I'll get all of you!" cries Sam-Cosmos, prancing about on his tree trunk: "Every last one of you! Just you come on then!"

The battle is a terrible one, and all the tyrannias are defeated by brave Cosmos. There they all lie, in the clearing, and Cosmos leaps forward, dancing his victory dance: "I won! I won!"

Then suddenly he stops. "Ohmigosh! My flute lesson! I forgot all about it!"

He picks up his bag, puts his hand in his pocket and,

"Oh! I've lost my money!" he cries, wide-eyed with horror.

The money to pay for his lesson. Miss Suzanne's money! Two five-dollar bills! He must have lost them during the great fight.

Sam searches the ground all around him; no money anywhere.

Sam feels more and more as if he were going to cry. He feels really miserable.

He turns his pocket out one more time. Maybe he has made a mistake. Maybe the money has been there all the time. Sadly,

It hasn't. He dares not think what his parents will say…and
on top of that he has made himself late because of the
tyrannias. With a heavy heart and dragging footsteps, he goes
on his way, but the forest has lost all its charm.

One of the things that Sam likes about Miss Suzanne is that she's even more scatterbrained than he is. When he arrives at her house, she is playing the piano, and waves to him to come in and sit down.

"There you are, Sam! My, you're so early today!"

Sam smiles at how scatterbrained the old lady is. Sam early! How absent-minded she is, really! So much the better, however.

"Sam," she goes on, "you haven't forgotten your flute today, have you? You can't do much without a flute, you know!"

"No, I've got it," answers Sam. He's afraid she may ask him, "Have you got your money?" But it doesn't seem to enter her mind. Miss Suzanne starts playing a musical phrase on the piano, and says to Sam, who has been listening to her very politely,

"Now it's your turn. Play this little flute tune."

Sam gradually relaxes and thinks about nothing except the music and the simple little tunes he's able to get out of his flute.

Suddenly his worry comes back. He gets up, ready to tell the whole story about the money. But just then the telephone rings, and Miss Suzanne goes to answer it, signaling to Sam that he may go. "Time's up, see you next time," she says, just as she picks up the telephone.

Sam wastes no time. "See you next Wednesday!" he says
and hurries away, only too pleased that Miss Suzanne
has forgotten to ask him for the money.

On the way home, Sam does not even once think about the tyrannias. He is sad and walks along taking little steps. "Where can that wretched money be?" he moans to himself.

When he gets to the clearing, he stops to have another careful look among the grass and leaves. Still nothing. At last he makes up his mind to go on home and tell his mother all about it. The sooner he tells her, the better he will feel.

The kitchen door is wide open. Sam sees Mama
checking something in the oven, and there is such a
good smell in the air!

"Hello," she says, catching sight of him: "Be a good boy,
Sam, and set the table quickly. Dad will be home soon
and I..."

"Mama," says Sam in a low voice, "You know, I...I've
lost..."

"What! What have you lost?" says Mama, seeing the tragic look on the boy's face, "Well, come on now! Say something, do!"

"I've lost the money for the lesson — the money you gave me!"

"The money I gave you?" Mama repeats, with a smile. "Oh, Sam, what a little scatterbrain you are! I didn't give you any money this morning! I ran into Miss Suzanne yesterday in town, and I paid her ahead of time."

"Ohmigosh!" cries Sam, surprised by such incredible news.

"What a hard time you've had, my poor Sam! I should have told you!"

"Yes, Mama, you certainly should have! But next time, give the money to me. I'll never lose it or forget it again."

"Well, we can try, if you like," replies Mama. "Tell me, does Captain Cosmos like cake?"

"Oh yes, that's for sure. Captain Cosmos is hungry.
As hungry as a tyrannia!!"